DINOSAURS
SPOT THE DIFFERENCES

Copyright ©2020 by Little McMike

Ready to play?
So let's START!

Spot the 5 differences.

Spot the 6 differences.

Spot the 5 differences.

Spot the 6 differences.

Spot the 6 differences.

Spot the 7 differences.

Spot the 5 differences.

Spot the 8 differences.

Spot the 6 differences.

Spot the 5 differences.

Spot the 6 differences.

Spot the 7 differences.

Spot the 5 differences.

Spot the 7 differences.

Spot the 6 differences.

Spot the 7 differences.

Spot the 6 differences.

Spot the 7 differences.

Spot the 6 differences.

Spot the 7 differences.

If You are satisfied with the book, I will be grateful if You could take a moment to submit a review.

Printed in Great Britain
by Amazon